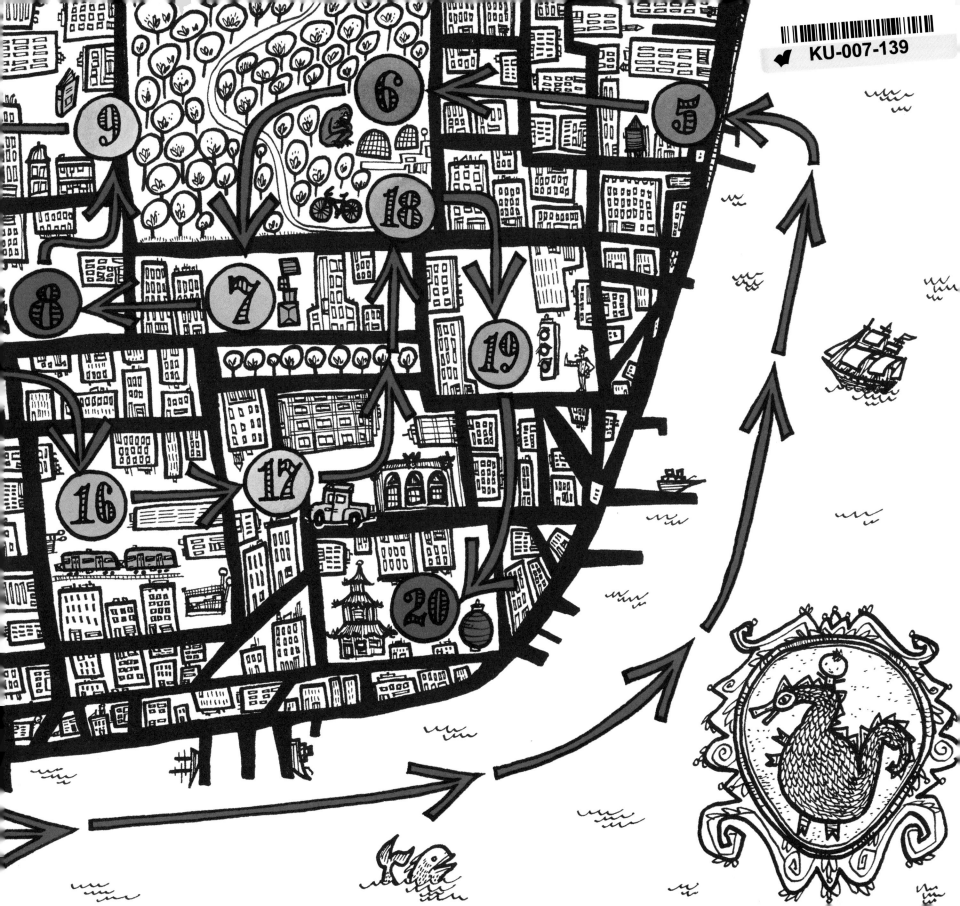

To Olive and Ivy — may the city always be your playground.

First published 2014 by Walker Books Ltd
87 Vauxhall Walk, London SE11 5HJ

This edition published 2015

3 4 5 6 7 8 9 10

© 2014 Steve Light

The right of Steve Light to be identified as author/illustrator of this work has been
asserted by him in accordance with the Copyright, Designs and Patents Act 1988

This book has been typeset in Stempel Schneidler

Printed in China

British Library Cataloguing in Publication Data: a catalogue
record for this book is available from the British Library

ISBN 978-1-4063-6063-9

www.walker.co.uk

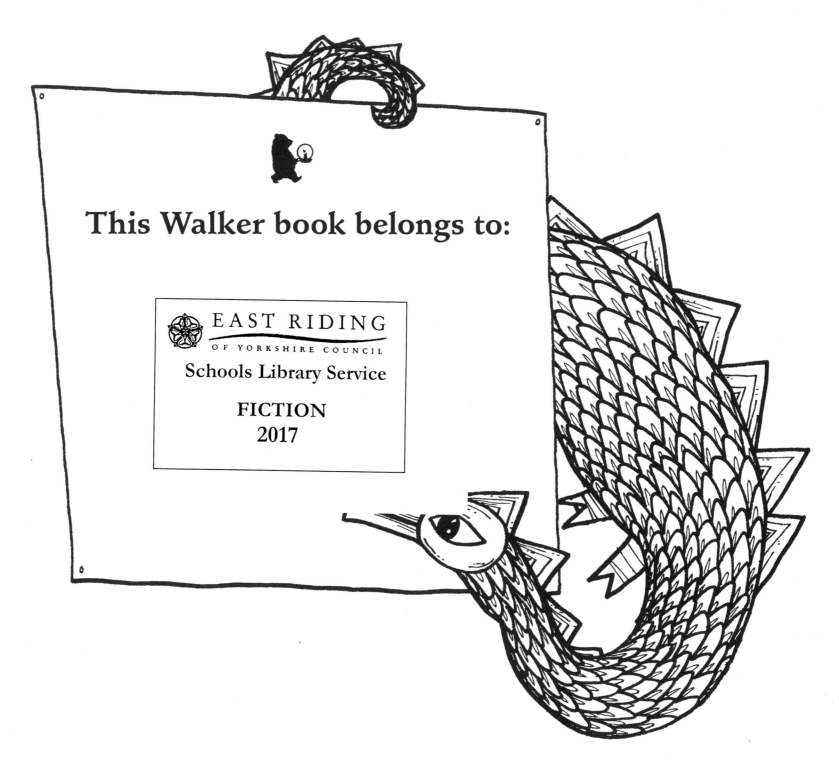

This Walker book belongs to:

EAST RIDING
OF YORKSHIRE COUNCIL

Schools Library Service

FICTION
2017

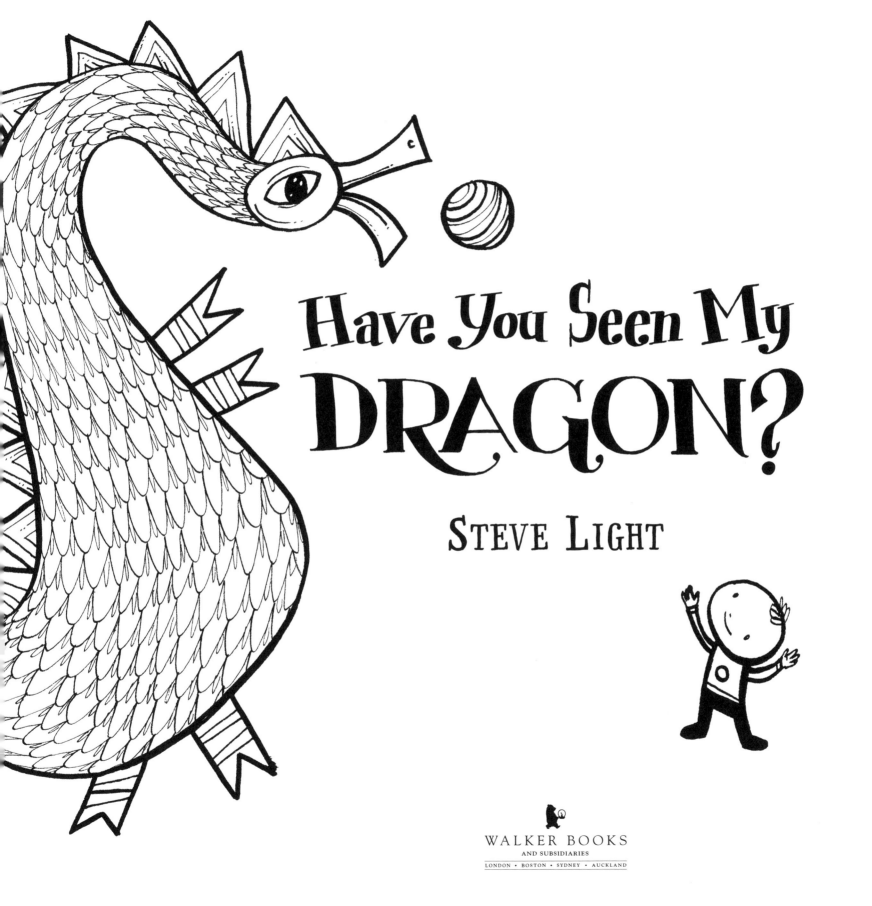

Have You Seen My DRAGON?

STEVE LIGHT

WALKER BOOKS
AND SUBSIDIARIES
LONDON · BOSTON · SYDNEY · AUCKLAND

Have you seen my dragon?

No? I will look for him.

Maybe he got hungry
and stopped for a hot dog.

Or perhaps he went into town on the bus.

It's possible
he went for
a swim.

4 Sailing ships

Or climbed up to get
a drink of water.

5 Water towers

Has my dragon been here
to visit the monkeys?

Could he be helping the delivery man again?

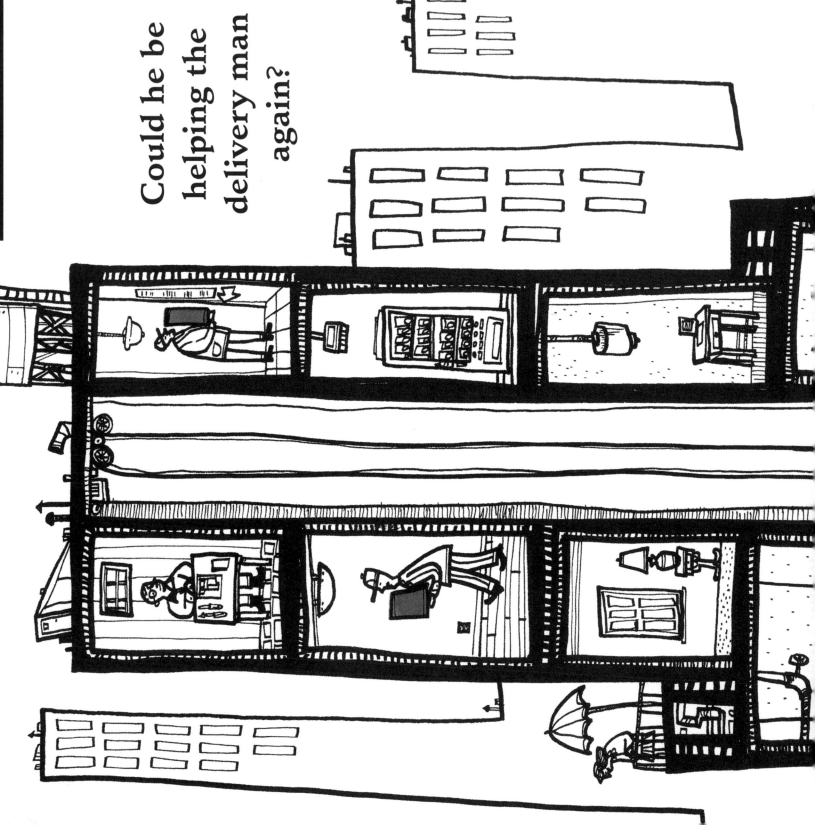

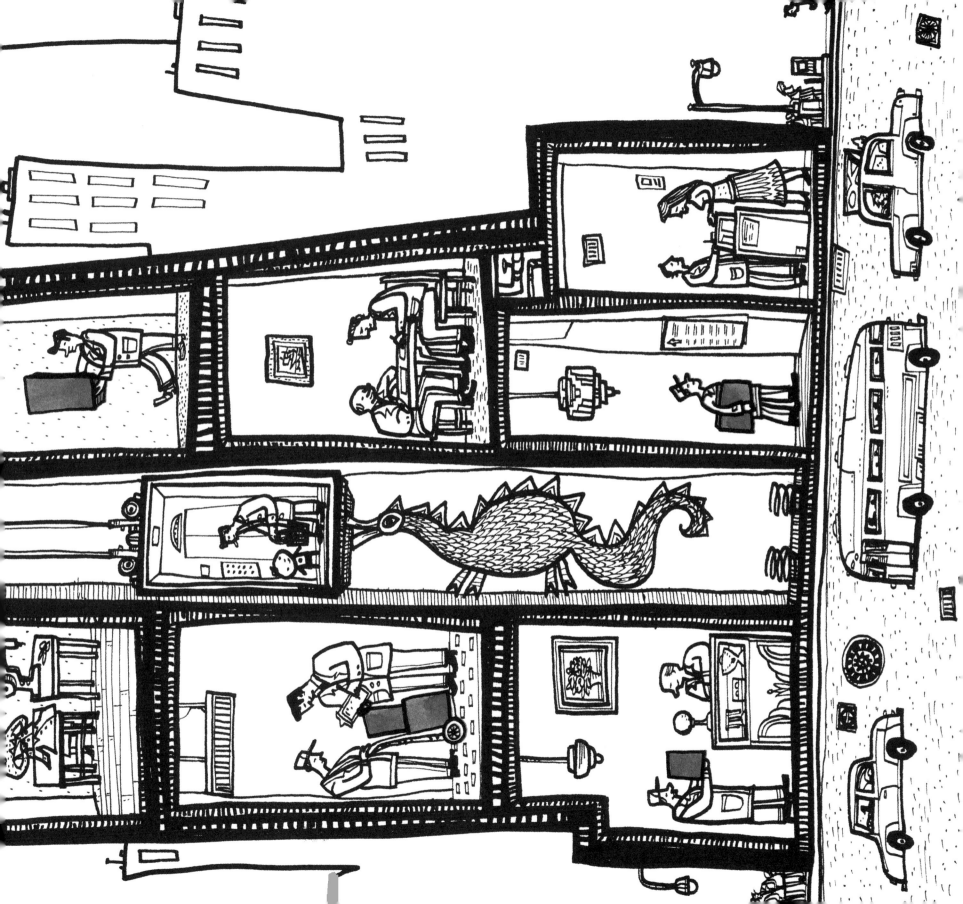

I hope he didn't start a fire with his dragon breath!

I will look at the book stall. My dragon loves to read.

Hello!
Has a dragon come through here?

Where could he be?
Down underground …

12 Pigeons

or up high
on a rooftop?

I want ice-cream!
Maybe my dragon wants some, too.

He loves the park ...

and especially the playground.
Maybe he's there!

Did he go under the town on a train ...

16 Carriages

or across town in a taxi?

Where is my dragon?

I've searched everywhere ... but wait! There's one more place to look.

There he is!
Right where I left him.

Steve Light is the author-illustrator of many books for children, including *Zephyr Takes Flight* and *Have You Seen My Monster?* When he is not writing or illustrating books he teaches at a nursery school. Steve Light lives in the USA, in New York City, with his wife and cat.

You might also enjoy:

ISBN 978-1-4063-4029-7

ISBN 978-1-4063-5943-5

Available from all good booksellers

www.walker.co.uk